Snow White
AND THE SEVEN DWARFS

retold by FREYA LITTLEDALE

Illustrated by SUSAN JEFFERS

SCHOLASTIC INC.
NEW YORK · TORONTO · LONDON · AUCKLAND · SYDNEY · TOKYO

ISBN 0-590-40685-X

12 11 10 9 8 7 6 5 4 3 2 1   6 7 8 9/8 0 1/9

Printed in the U.S.A.   24

Once upon a time, in the middle of winter,

a queen sat sewing at a window.

Snowflakes were falling

like feathers from the sky.

As the queen watched the snowflakes,

she pricked her finger with the needle.

And three drops of red blood fell on the white snow.

"How pretty those colors are," thought the queen.

"If only I had a daughter

as white as snow, as red as blood,

and as black as the ebony wood on this window."

It was not long
before the queen did have a daughter.
The little girl was as white as snow.
Her lips were red as blood.
And her hair was as black as ebony.
The queen called the child Snow White.

But the queen died after Snow White was born,
and, in time, the king married again.

The new queen was beautiful.
But she was proud and vain.
She couldn't bear to think that anyone
might be more beautiful than she.

Every day the queen went to a
magic mirror and said:

> "Mirror, mirror, on the wall,
> Who is the fairest one of all?"

And the magic mirror answered:

> "You are the fairest one of all."

But Snow White grew more beautiful each year.
And one day when the queen said:

> "Mirror, mirror, on the wall,
> Who is the fairest one of all?"

the magic mirror answered:

> "Oh, queen, you are fair, it's true,
> But Snow White is far more fair than you."

From that moment on
the queen hated Snow White.
She hated her more and more every day.

At last she called her huntsman and said,
"Take Snow White into the woods and kill her!
And bring me her heart to prove you have done it!"

The huntsman took Snow White
deep into the woods.
But when he pulled out his knife to kill her,
Snow White began to cry.
"Oh, dear huntsman, do not kill me!
I will go far away
and never come home again."

The huntsman took pity on her and said,
"All right, poor child, run away."
"The wild animals will eat her soon enough," he thought.
"I do not have to kill her myself."

Just then a wild boar jumped out of the bushes.
The huntsman killed the wild boar
and took its heart to the queen.
Then the wicked woman was happy
because she thought Snow White was dead.

Snow White was running through the woods.
It was getting dark.
The wind howled through the trees,
and wild animals were all around.
The animals did not harm her,
but Snow White was afraid.
She ran as fast as she could.

Just when she thought she could
not run another step,
Snow White saw a little house
by the side of a hill,
and she went inside to rest.

Everything in the house was very small
and as neat as could be.
A little table was set for supper
with seven knives and forks,
seven bowls and cups,
and seven little loaves of bread.
And near the wall stood seven little beds
all in a row.

Snow White was so tired,
she lay down on one of the beds
and fell asleep.

Now, the house belonged
to seven dwarfs
who worked in the hills
digging for gold.

That night when the seven dwarfs came home,
they lit their seven candles
and saw Snow White sleeping.
"Oh, my!" they cried.
"How beautiful she is!"
And they were careful
not to wake her.

In the morning they asked her
how she came to their cottage,
and Snow White told them all about the wicked queen.

"If you will help us cook and clean,
you may stay with us," the dwarfs said.
"But you must remember one thing.
When we are at work don't let anyone in.
The wicked queen will soon learn
you are here."

"I'll remember," said Snow White.

"Good," said the dwarfs.
And they went off to the hills to dig for gold.

That very morning
the queen looked into her magic mirror and said:

> *"Mirror, mirror, on the wall,*
> *Who is the fairest one of all?"*

And the magic mirror answered:

> *"Oh, queen, you are fair, it's true,*
> *But Snow White is far more fair than you.*
> *Near the hill where seven dwarfs dwell,*
> *Snow White is still alive and well."*

Then the queen knew
the huntsman had fooled her.
She was very angry.
"I will kill Snow White myself," she thought,
"and be rid of her forever!"

The wicked queen changed her clothes
and painted her face.
She made herself look like an old woman.

No one would have guessed who she was.
Then she went through the woods
and came to the hill
where she found the home of the seven dwarfs.

"Buckles and laces for sale!" she called.
"Pretty buckles and laces!"
And she held up a lace
of bright red silk.

Snow White peeped through the window.
"Just an old woman selling laces," she thought.
"Surely it's safe to let her in."

So Snow White opened the door
for the wicked queen.
"Here's a pretty silk lace for you," the queen said.
"Come, my dear, and I will tie it nicely."

But the queen tied the lace so tightly
it took Snow White's breath away.
And she fell to the floor
as if she were dead.
"Now *I'm* the fairest in the land!" said the queen.
And she hurried away.

When the seven dwarfs came home
they found Snow White on the floor.
Quickly they cut the lace
and Snow White began to breathe again.
She told them about the old woman.
"That was not an old woman," said the dwarfs.
"That was the wicked queen!
You must not let strangers in
no matter what they look like."

As soon as the queen was back at the palace,
she went to her magic mirror and said:
>"Mirror, mirror, on the wall,
>Who is the fairest one of all?"

And the magic mirror answered:
>"Oh, queen, you are fair, it's true,
>But Snow White is far more fair than you.
>Near the hill where seven dwarfs dwell,
>Snow White is still alive and well."

The wicked queen turned pale with anger.
"The dwarfs must have saved her!" she cried.
And she thought of another plan
to kill Snow White.

First she made a poisoned comb.
Then she dressed like a different old woman.
And off she went to the home of the seven dwarfs.

"Combs for sale!" she called.
"Pretty combs for sale!"

Snow White looked out of the window
and saw an old woman dressed in rags.
She felt sorry for her.
But she remembered what the dwarfs had said.
"I don't know you," she called.
"You must go away."

"Look at this pretty comb," said the queen.
"Just open the door a little
and I will give it to you."

"Surely there's no harm in that," thought Snow White.
So she opened the door a little
and took the pretty comb.

But as soon as she combed her hair
the poison began to work.
And Snow White fell down
as if she were dead.

"There! That's the end of you!" said the queen.
And she hurried away.

When the dwarfs came home
they saw Snow White on the floor.
Quickly they found the poisoned comb
and took it from her hair.
Snow White opened her eyes.
She told the dwarfs what had happened.
"That was the wicked queen again," the dwarfs said.
"You must not open the door to strangers."

As soon as the queen was back at the palace
she ran to the magic mirror and said:

> "*Mirror, mirror, on the wall,*
> *Who is the fairest one of all?*"

And the magic mirror answered:

> "*Oh, queen, you are fair, it's true,*
> *But Snow White is far more fair than you.*
> *Near the hill where seven dwarfs dwell,*
> *Snow White is still alive and well.*"

The queen turned purple with rage.
"Snow White must die!" she cried.
"This time there will be no mistake!"

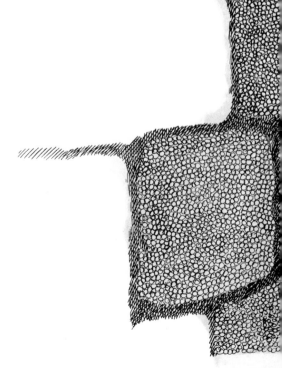

She went into a secret room.
There she made a poison so powerful
it could kill in an instant.
Then she took an apple that was so beautiful
anyone would want to eat it.
Half of the apple was red
and half was yellow.
Carefully, the queen put poison
in the red half of the apple.
"Now it's ready for Snow White!" said she.

Then the queen painted wrinkles on her face.
She dressed all in black and leaned on a cane.
And off she went to the home of the seven dwarfs.
"Apples for sale!" she called.
"Juicy apples for sale!"

Snow White looked out of the window and said,
"Go away, please! I must not let anyone in."

"You don't have to let me in," said the queen.

"Just open the window,
and I will give you this beautiful apple."
"No!" said Snow White.

"What's wrong, my dear?" said the queen.
"Do you think it's poisoned?
Look! I will cut the apple in two pieces
and eat half of it myself."
Then the wicked queen ate the yellow half
and gave the poisoned half to Snow White.

No sooner did Snow White take a bite
than she fell dead to the floor.

The wicked queen laughed.
"The seven dwarfs can't save you now!" she said.

As soon as the queen reached the palace
she ran to the magic mirror:

"Mirror, mirror, on the wall,
Who is the fairest one of all?"

And the magic mirror answered:

"You are the fairest one of all."

At last the queen was happy
for the magic mirror never lied.

That evening when the seven dwarfs came home,
they saw that Snow White was dead.
There was nothing they could do to save her.

"This time we're too late!" they cried.
"The queen has killed Snow White!"
And they sat beside her and wept
for three days and three nights.

Snow White looked so beautiful and alive,
they couldn't bear to put her in the cold ground.
They built a coffin of glass for her.
And they printed her name in gold.
Under her name they wrote: PRINCESS.
Then they put the coffin on the hilltop
where they could always watch over it.

One morning a prince rode
through the woods with his men.
He stopped on the hilltop
and he saw the glass coffin.
Snow White looked as if she were sleeping.

"She is so beautiful!" said the prince.
"If only I could look at her always!
Please let me take her with me," he asked the dwarfs.
"I will give you anything you want."

"No," said the dwarfs.
But the prince grew so sad
the dwarfs felt sorry for him.
And at last they agreed to let him
take Snow White away.

Then the prince told his men
to carry the glass coffin on their shoulders.
But as the men were walking
they tripped over a rock,
and the piece of poisoned apple fell out of Snow White's mouth.

Snow White opened her eyes.
"Where am I?" she cried.

"You are safe with me," said the prince.
And he told her all that had happened.
"Come with me and be my wife!"

"I will!" said Snow White.
And they rode off together
to the prince's palace.

Everyone was invited to the wedding —
even the wicked queen.

The queen put on her finest gown
and she wore her finest jewels.
Then she went to the magic mirror and said:

> "*Mirror, mirror, on the wall,*
> *Who is the fairest one of all?*"

And the magic mirror answered:

> "*Oh, queen, you are fair, it's true,*
> *But the young bride is far more fair than you.*"

"No! No!" the queen shouted.
"That can't be true!
I must see the bride for myself!"
And she rushed off to the wedding.

When she entered the palace and saw Snow White,
the queen choked with rage and fell dead to the floor.

Snow White and the prince lived happily forever after.